DOCTOR·WHO

THE SYCORAX

BBC CHILDREN'S BOOKS
Published by the Penguin Group
Penguin Books Ltd, 80 Strand, London, WC2R 0RL, England
Penguin Group (USA), Inc., 375 Hudson Street, New York, New York 10014, USA
Penguin Books (Australia) Ltd, 250 Camberwell Road, Camberwell, Victoria 3124, Australia.
(A division of Pearson Australia Group Pty Ltd)
Canada, India, New Zealand, South Africa.
Published by BBC Children's Books, 2006
Text and design © Children's Character Books, 2006.
Written by Jacqueline Rayner. The Final Darkness by Stephen Cole.
10 9 8 7 6 5 4 3 2 1
Printed in China.
ISBN-13: 978-1-40590-248-9
ISBN-10: 1-40590-248-5

CONTENTS

Meet the Sycorax

Introduction......................................4

Sycorax Data....................................6

Sycorax Anatomy.............................8

⬢ Test your Knowledge

History of the Sycorax

History of the Sycorax....................10

⬢ Test your Knowledge

Enemies and Rivals

Rose...14

The Doctor......................................15

Harriet Jones..................................16

Torchwood......................................17

⬢ Test your Knowledge

No Place Like Home

'Pilot Fish' Aliens............................18

Sycoraxic..20

⬢ Test your Knowledge

Weapons and Technology

Weaponry..22

Blood Control..................................24

Messages to Aliens..........................25

⬢ Test your Knowledge

The Christmas Invasion

The Christmas Invasion..............26

⬢ Test your Knowledge

Test your Knowledge Answers........30

The Final Darkness

The Final Darkness..................31

MEET THE SYCORAX

The scavenging Sycorax travel through space searching for worlds to ransack. Planets which are taking their first steps into space are ideal targets for the Sycorax, as they usually have a suitably advanced level of technology to make attacking them worthwhile, but not so high as to make them able to withstand an invasion.

Ritual and superstition play a large part in the Sycorax way of life and since they have embraced technology they can guarantee that their spells and curses really work. Blood and bones play a large part in Sycorax ceremonies. The rite of blood control is a particular favourite, guaranteed to spread fear and panic in the Sycorax's victims.

The Sycorax are a warlike people, although they prefer to subjugate a planet with no resistance, their love of fighting means they will not turn away from combat. Single combat, with its rules and rituals, appeals to their warrior spirit, but their desire for victory at any price often wins out over honour.

POLICE PUBLIC BO

Name: The Sycorax

Height: approx. 1.90m (6'2")

Skin: Muscle and bone

Eyes: Red

Home planet: Sycorax

Language: Sycoraxic

Profession: Scavengers

SYCORAX ANATOMY

Skull helmet to inspire fear.

Red eyes that glow

Trophies from conquests

Totems and decorations on staff show tribe and tribal status

Blood–red velvet robe indicates wealth

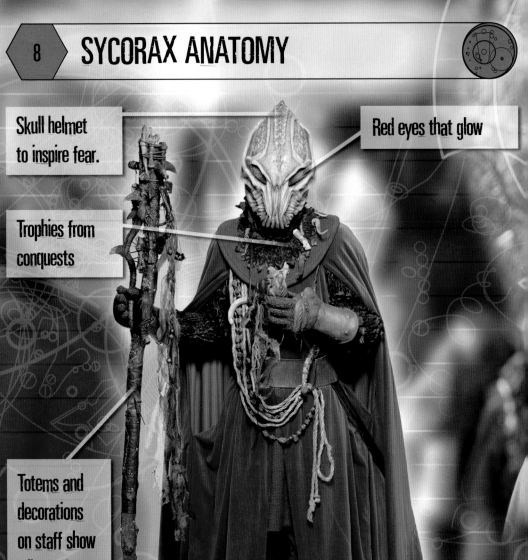

TEST YOUR KNOWLEDGE

The Sycorax come from a distant planet, far out in the wastelands of the galaxy. Nobody on Earth was aware of its existence, until one fateful Christmas day...

The many tribes of the Sycorax lived just beneath the surface of a small asteroid that was composed mainly of rock and ice. This inhospitable world had few natural resources, but the warlike Sycorax forged an existence there, tribe fighting tribe for scraps of food and metal. These primitive Sycorax worshipped Astrophia, goddess of darkness and death, each tribe trying to outdo the others in reverence and offerings. Sycorax shamen, the tribal wise men, carried out rites of blood and sacrifice to implore Astrophia to bring favour to their tribes and misfortune to others in battle.

After many centuries of tribal conflict, the Sycorax became aware of the existence of other beings in the universe. A spaceship crash-landed on the surface of their world, bringing them into contact with another species for the first time. The Halvinor Tribe enslaved the survivors, and forced them to teach the Sycorax of their technology. This threatened to bring terrible war to the Sycorax, as the other tribes both resented and feared the Halvinor's discovery. But the shaman of the Halvinor persuaded them that instead of fighting among themselves, the Sycorax should unite in order to exploit the newly discovered universe, so full of riches.

Working together, the Sycorax developed their new-found technology. With little metal on their planet, they hit on an ambitious plan — to pilot the tiny asteroid from world to world, plundering their wealth and enslaving their people. This they did for many generations, growing richer and richer, until finally the mechanism controlling the travel systems failed and the asteroid became trapped in the orbit of a planet at the far outer reaches of our solar system. But the Sycorax refused to give up their space-scavenging ways and return to a life of hardship.

THE DOCTOR

It was straight back to work for the Doctor, who woke up from his regenerative coma to find himself in the middle of an invasion. But if the Sycorax thought they'd get an easy ride from the recovering Time Lord, they were mistaken. After removing the threat of the Sycorax's blood control, the Doctor stood as champion of the Earth and challenged the leader of the Sycorax to single combat — with the planet as the prize. The Doctor won, but the Sycorax Leader proved he was not to be trusted when he attempted to kill the Doctor after the combat had ended.

HARRIET JONES

Since Harriet Jones met the Slitheen during their invasion of 10 Downing Street, she's known that the Earth faces a serious threat from extraterrestrials — and she knows that the Doctor won't always be on hand to save the day. As Prime Minister she attempted to negotiate with the Sycorax following their threats and refused to surrender the planet to them. When there was no sign of the Doctor she called on Torchwood, hoping they would be able to destroy the aliens.

TORCHWOOD

Torchwood is one of the
most secret organisations
on Earth, even the
British Prime Minister
isn't supposed to
know about it.
The Torchwood
Institute was founded
by Queen Victoria
to investigate strange
and alien happenings.
It has links with UNIT, a
military organisation that deals
with alien threats, although the
existence of Torchwood has been
kept from the UN itself. Torchwood
collects alien technology that comes to
Earth and adapts it for their own use, such
as defending the planet. The weapon that
destroyed the Sycorax ship had been adapted
from alien technology, from a ship that had fallen
to Earth ten years before.

TEST YOUR KNOWLEDGE

'PILOT FISH' ALIENS

In nature, 'pilot fish' swim with much more powerful sharks, knowing they'll be led to food. The robotic space 'pilot fish' aliens keep close to fearsome space travellers such as the Sycorax, who will lead them to energy-rich planets. As the Sycorax focused on Earth, the 'pilot fish' aliens that travelled alongside them detected the Doctor's regenerative energy and hijacked the Sycorax's teleportation technology to track him down. The 'pilot fish' aliens tried to take out the Doctor's defences, first by disguising themselves as Santa Clauses and attacking Rose and Mickey, then by sending a remote-controlled homicidal Christmas tree to Jackie's flat. With his defenders out of the way, it would have been easier to steal the Doctor's energy — a power source large enough to feed the pilot fish for several years.

WEAPONS

Disguised as a carol-playing brass trio, the robots caused mayhem with their deadly instruments, making sure it wasn't a *Silent Night* for Rose and Mickey.

Trombone of Terror
really a flame thrower!

Tricky Trumpet
a machine gun in disguise!

Terrible Tuba acts as a missile launcher!

SYCORAXIC

Harriet Jones and her team needed a computer to translate the Sycorax's language into English, but this handy guide to Sycoraxic words and phrases should make things easier next time the Sycorax try to invade the Earth!

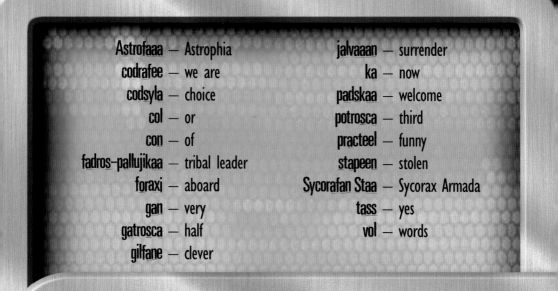

Astrofaaa — Astrophia	jalvaaan — surrender
codrafee — we are	ka — now
codsyla — choice	padskaa — welcome
col — or	potrosca — third
con — of	practeel — funny
fadros-pallujikaa — tribal leader	stapeen — stolen
foraxi — aboard	Sycorafan Staa — Sycorax Armada
gan — very	tass — yes
gatrosca — half	vol — words
gilfane — clever	

Tass, conafee tedro soo — Yes, we know who you are.

Sycora jak! Sycora telpo! Sycora faa! — Sycorax strong! Sycorax mighty! Sycorax rock!

Jalvaaan, col chack chiff — Surrender, or they will die.

Crel stat foraxi — Bring it on board.

Codrafee Sycora. Codrafee gassac tel dashfellik — We are the Sycorax. We stride the darkness.

WHIP

The Sycorax whip is one of the most fearsome weapons in existence, causing immediate death. A single touch of the whiplash instantaneously disintegrates every atom of human flesh, leaving only a burnt skeleton. The Sycorax use this to punish prisoners or inspire fear rather than in a combat situation.

STAFF

The Sycorax's staff may be used as a weapon, but it has another important function. The totems which adorn the staff indicate tribal allegiance, while the trophies and decorations show the status within the tribe of the Sycorax who wields it. Destroying the staff of a Sycorax is a terrible insult, implying that they are not worthy of the position they claim.

BLOOD CONTROL

When the Sycorax took the Guinevere One probe on to their ship, they discovered a plaque which was intended to identify the human race to any aliens who might encounter it. The probe contained maps, music, wheat seeds, water, and A+ human blood. The Sycorax used the blood to feed a control matrix, which gave them power over everyone on Earth who had that blood type.

Types of blood are usually sorted into groups according to the ABO system and the Rhesus (Rh) system, depending on what antigens they contain.

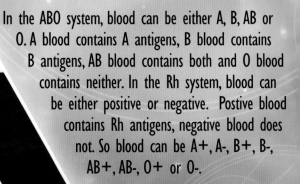

In the ABO system, blood can be either A, B, AB or O. A blood contains A antigens, B blood contains B antigens, AB blood contains both and O blood contains neither. In the Rh system, blood can be either positive or negative. Postive blood contains Rh antigens, negative blood does not. So blood can be A+, A-, B+, B-, AB+, AB-, O+ or O-.

About one third of the people on Earth have A+ blood. Do you know what type you have? Would the Sycorax have been able to control you?

Rose begged the unconscious Doctor for his help and he woke long enough to save everyone. But before he collapsed again he warned them that the robots were just 'pilot fish' aliens after his energy. Something much worse was coming.

An image was beamed to Earth from Guinevere One — a terrifying alien face. UNIT detected a ship heading towards the Earth, and the alien Sycorax demanded the surrender of Earth's people. Prime Minster Harriet Jones refused.

The Sycorax took control of everyone on Earth whose blood type is A+, and sent them to the edge of the highest point they could reach. If the Sycorax didn't get what they wanted, they would make the people jump. Mickey and Rose took shelter in the TARDIS, taking the Doctor with them.

Prime Minister Harriet Jones and her colleagues were teleported aboard the Sycorax ship and so was the TARDIS. Rose tried to face up to the Sycorax, but just as all hope seemed to be lost, the TARDIS door opened. The Doctor was back, reinvigorated by tea!

The Doctor activated the Sycorax's blood control matrix, but no one jumped. The human instinct for survival is too strong. With the threat removed, the Doctor challenged the Sycorax leader to single combat, to decide ownership of the planet.

The fight was fierce. The Doctor was knocked over and the Sycorax leader cut off his hand! But the Doctor had enough residual cellular energy from his regeneration to grow a new one. He continued the fight and the Sycorax leader was defeated.

THE FINAL DARKNESS

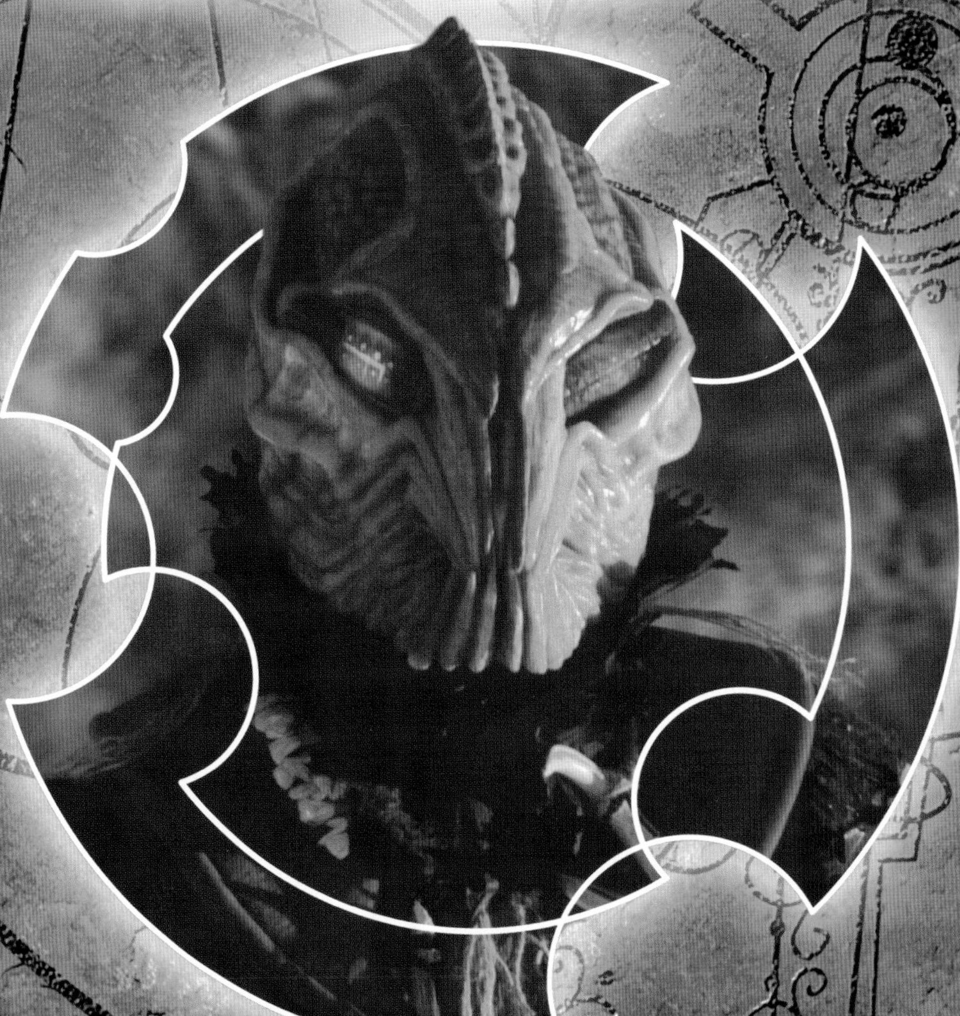

Journal of the Ship's Scribe

(Translation © UNIT Alien-English software)

Entry: 23-mol-786-lassac-5

Sycorax stride the darkness. The wastelands of space are our home. And this day, signals came to us from a newfound planet.

"Its people are soft and fleshy and primitive," the world-seer reported. "They call themselves humans and send sounds and pictures to each other through the air. They send tiny metal probes into the darkness between the stars."

"What is the planet called?" our leader asked.

"They name it Earth, after mud," said the world-seer. "But even so far away, I taste its true value. I sense the precious stones beneath its surface. The metals and minerals."

Our leader thought on the world-seer's report. "Slave traders will give us much for a good supply of human cattle. Let us go to this world and take whatever we wish."

Soon I felt the tremble of the ground
as our ship turned through the blankness
of far space. Our instruments are
locked on to the source of the signals.
The Earth shall be our next target –
our next jewel plucked from
the glittering heavens.

Entry: 24-mol-853-

lassac-21

Our long move through
the stars is filled now
with anticipation.
We pass the orbits
of comets and dust

clouds and draw close to the system of Earth.

Entry: 24-mol-921-lassac-13

As we neared the small red planet in the system of Earth, our sensors detected a tiny metal object approaching.

"It is a probe sent by the human cattle," our wise men declared.

"Do they know we are coming?" our leader asked. "Are they sending weapons to attack?

We stopped five *kiskfaa* above the red planet and our ship swallowed the probe. Many of our wise men studied it.

"It is rubbish," the eldest declared. "It carries a big camera, and is meant to send fuzzy pictures to the cattle of Earth."

"It also contains things from their planet," his comrade added. "Seeds, fluid, maps. A bad noise that may be music. And something that will be of use to us – human blood."

And so, swiftly, our shamen – they who practice the forbidden arts of Astrophia – began to prepare the blood charm. While they worked, our leader put on his skull helmet and stared into the fuzzy camera of the probe. As it sent the image to the people of Earth, he snapped his mighty teeth like he was biting off their heads!

Ha, ha, ha, we know how to scare the human cattle!

Sycorax rock!

Entry: 24-mol-921-lassac-18

Our ship slices through space. In five human hours our ship shall reach the Earth. To pass time, our leader sends a message to the human cattle's tribal leader. He demands total surrender. He does not speak the language of humans. Such stupid words would taste like dung in his mouth. We speak Sycoraxic and do not care if the humans cannot understand us – we shall take what we want from them whatever they say about it. Ha! Sycorax strong!

Entry: 24-mol-921-lassac-20/22

The human cattle have learnt Sycoraxic. They say they have weapons. They say, "We do not surrender."

We say— "HA! SYCORAX MIGHTY!" Our leader has cast the charm of blood control over all the planet Earth.

Now one third of all human scum are compelled to climb high buildings and stand on the brink of falling down-ness.

Of course, it is all big trick. Blood control will not kill even stupid human cattle. But they do not know this.

Ha ha! Our tribe love conquest by blood control best – it totally rocks because it is very funny to make fools of enemies. Once we have gathered half the people of Earth we shall tell them their leader gave in for nothing and laugh at them and shut them in the dark until we are ready to trade them for goods and money and *slinkjaak*.

Entry: 24-mol-921-lassac-20/22

Our leader summoned the skinny woman ruler of Earth, her chief warrior and her wise men to our ship. We, the tribe, have all gathered in the Hall of War Pacts to help him scare the cattle. They smell bad and look worse.

Our leader takes off his skull helmet, he rattles the bones of those he killed in childhood. We see the fear in the eyes of these human animals and it is good.

We scream and shout at them: Surrender! Surrender! Surrender!

ZZ-ZZAP! Our leader kills one of the woman's wise men because he is soft and boring. The wise man wants to see compassion – so our leader shows him his death whip. ZZ-ZZAAAPPP! Ha! He kills the skinny woman's dark warrior too, who is rubbish and dies just like that.

And then he tells the skinny woman who rules these humans – surrender half your people to be slaves, or watch a third of them jump and die. "Your choice!"

Except we are tricking her.

I am glad I am wearing my skull helmet because I cannot stop smiling.

Entry: 24-mol-921-lassac-22.6

ALARM! Our controls taste the signals of FOREIGN MACHINERY. Machinery not made on this world. Clever machinery.

Are the humans hiding something dangerous? Are they conspiring with intelligent strangers? Do they seek to trick us?

Our teleportation beam locks on to

the clever machine and brings it aboard. It is a blue wooden box. It does not look clever, but it is. Two humans fall out of it. A yellow girl and a dark boy.

Our leader talks to the yellow girl. It seems the clever blue box is hers. Our leader says she must speak for the Earth.

But the yellow girl speaks without logic.

She is not clever like her blue box. She tries to scare us with stolen words. She tries to make us afraid by using the names of worthy foes. Does she not know she speaks to SYCORAX? We who inhabit the great blackness between stars? We who stride the darkness eternal?

We laugh till we leak. The yellow girl looks afraid, and so she should. For our leader has drawn his death whip. He will destroy her...

But then the doors of the blue box burst open. And a stranger appears.

A stranger who pulls the death whip from our leader's hands, and who breaks the Staff of Helkaac-ak-ac across his knee.

We do not understand but we know it is bad, and we do not laugh now.

Entry: 24-mol-921-lassac-24

The unthinkable has happened.

The stranger – whose rank is DOCTOR – has activated the blood control matrix and ruined EVERYTHING. The human cattle far below are freed from the blood charm and return to their feeble senses. Sycorax no longer control them. They stand back from the edges and ledges of their high buildings.

It is bad.

Now, we the tribe wait and anticipate. We know our leader will desire a great and sour revenge for this act.

And so, when the Doctor invokes the sanctified rules of combat and stands as Champion of Earth... When he dares to challenge our leader

to fight for possession of this planet... When he calls our leader a *crannak pel cassackree salvack* before the chimes of darkness are even rung...

We know our leader will crush him like a *salvsqueed* beneath his boot.

The ship rocks with our cheers and bellows. For time unknown we have conquered and enslaved, we have gutted planets and left them empty and dry behind us.

And never once have we seen such sport as this – a pink and puny fool, fighting our own glorious leader!

Our Leader and the Doctor fight across the hall with heavy broadswords. The struggle spills outside onto the wing of our ship. But even with the filthy air of this world filling his lungs, we know our leader will surely triumph...

It is certain! Sycorax ROCK!

I scramble down from the upper gallery to see. As scribe of the ship it is my duty to record such momentous events. But even if I were lowly as a *dalskaak* I would be running to watch this battle. For my eyes long to see the blood spurt from this Doctor's body. My heart aches to see the champion of this world humbled and hacked into chunks, hurled at the planet below – the planet that shall soon be OURS to pillage!

Sure enough, our leader soon shows his superior skill. He brings down his broadsword and slices off the Doctor's fighting hand!

Earth's champion has shown guts, but now our leader will tug them out with his bare hands...

And then, suddenly I feel a stab of purest fear deep inside. I have not known fear since I was first torn as a pup from the belly of my father and thrown to the snake baths of Hennteck. But I know it now.

For this hero of the humans, the Doctor, knows true witchcraft. His severed hand grows back, and in seconds it is whole and strong again! And now, as if a man renewed, this Doctor fights with a fury greater than any I have ever seen. He swings and blocks and clashes and knocks the broadsword flying from the hands of our leader.

Our leader falls to the floor. I feel a cold as deep as the wastelands of space in my heart.

He is at the Doctor's mercy. He waits for death.

But the Doctor will not kill him. He commands him to leave this planet and never return. Our leader agrees – but it is a trick. Ha, ha – a good trick, yes! He rises, comes up behind the Doctor, ready to kill the

presumptuous fool, to kill—

—himself.

Without even looking, the Doctor triggers the *kojux*-flap in the wing of the ship. Our leader tumbles through it. He plummets to the ground miles below.

But my heart plummets faster.

Entry: 24-mol-921-lassac-28

We are leaving now, in disarray. Leaderless. More alone than we ever have been as we return to the endless, open void.

We have been forbidden to scavenge the Earth for the rest of time. We are compelled to inform the great Sycorax Armada that this world is defended. It may not be taken. Bound by the ancient rites of combat, with our blood charms broken and our great leader gone to the Glorious Plains of Haansak-Chack-Chiffal, we cannot fight back. Not this day.

But still we shall stride the darkness. We know nothing else.

We leave for the wilderness beyond Mutter's Spiral. It is this scribe's one hope that the freezing wastes of far space will help to soothe the burning, bitter blackness in our hearts at this defeat.

Entry: 24-mol-921-lassac-28.910

Treachery. Deception. More clever, foreign machinery hidden on the Earth. Our sensors detect the energy streaming from the human mire towards our beautiful ship. And we know at once we cannot withstand it.

I stand and speak to our assembly in these last seconds. "We, who have travelled in the wastelands all our lives," I cry, "we know now that in death we shall remain here. We shall fill the darkness with our blood, with our curse, with our hate, with our vengeance. "

My brothers cheer my words as the deadly energy streaks nearer.

"Our armada shall scent our blood," I bellow. "It shall feel the burning of our hearts and be drawn here to wreak destruction on the Earth!"

And the chant goes up:

"SYCORAX STRONG! SYCORAX MIGHTY! SYCORAX——

+++LOG TERMINATES

DOCTOR · WHO

OTHER GREAT FILES TO COLLECT

1 The Doctor

2 Rose

3 The Slitheen

4 The Sycorax

5 Mickey

6 K-9

7 The Daleks

8 The Cybermen